Love Is What You Do

by Lisa Combs • illustrated by Pam Fraizer

Dedicated to the Wildlife Warriors
at the Australia Zoo Wildlife Hospital who have acted out their love
for our beautiful earth, in the rescue and rehabilitation
of tens of thousands of precious, unique animals.

"I have no fear of losing my life. If I have to save a koala or a crocodile or a kangaroo or a snake, mate, I will save it." — Steve Irwin

No part of this publication may be reproduced
in whole or part, or stored in a retrieval system,
or transmitted in any form, or by any means,
electronic, mechanical, photocopying, recording, or otherwise,
without written permission of the author and illustrator.

ISBN-13: 9781657606784

© 2020, Best Friend Books, LLC

Printed in the USA.

Love Is What You Do

by Lisa Combs • illustrated by Pam Fraizer

Quokka

I can say I love you.
You can say you love me too!
But love is more than what you say.
Love is what you DO.

Love is checking in to see
If a friend is feeling blue.
Love is more than what you say.
Love is what you DO.

Emu

Love is only saying things
That are thoughtful, kind and true.
Love is more than what you say.
Love is what you DO.

Love is more than what you say.
Love is what you DO.

Platypus

Love is making chicken soup,
For someone with the flu.
Love is more than what you say.
Love is what you DO.

Love is fixing someone's toy,
So it works just like brand new!
Love is more than what you say.
Love is what you DO.

Love is helping someone learn
With a timely, helpful clue.
Love is more than what you say.
Love is what you do.

Wombats

Love is filling an empty tummy
With a bowl of yummy stew.
Love is more than what you say.
Love is what you do.

Love is sharing pennies
With someone who has few.
Love is more than what you say.
Love is what you do.

Koala

Love is seeing a broken heart
And offering some glue.
Love is more than what you say.
Love is what you do.

Short Beaked Echidna

Kookaburras

Love is giving someone
An apology that's overdue.
Love is more than what you say.
Love is what you do.

Love is offering a friend
Your seat with a better view.
Love is more than what you say.
Love is what you do.

Kangaroos

Numbat

Love is donating clothing
That you long ago outgrew.
Love is more than what you say.
Love is what you do.

Love is planting a single tree
Where a giant forest once grew.
Love is more than what you say.
Love is what you do.

Bilby

It's easy to say "I love you,"
Or to reply, "I love you, too!"
But love is more than what you say.
Love is what you DO.

Koala

Lisa Combs

Lisa Combs is an author, university instructor, national speaker, and educational consultant specializing in programs for children with special needs. Throughout her career, she has had extensive experience with classroom instruction, academic and behavioral intervention, program development, mediation, job embedded coaching for evidence based practices and grant management ranging from public preschool to alternative school programs for at risk teens. Her passions include supporting children with autism, facilitating inclusive practices and supporting the social emotional development of young children.

To learn more about Lisa, visit her website at
www.combseducationalconsulting.com

Pam Fraizer

Pam Fraizer is a graphic artist, illustrator, and owner of FraizerDesigns, LLC.

To learn more about Pam, visit her website at
www.fraizerdesigns.org

Visit us both at www.bestfriendbooks.com

Made in the USA
Coppell, TX
21 October 2020